GALAXY ZACK

A HAUNTED HALLOWEEN

By Ray O'Ryan

Illustrated by Jason Kraft

LITTLE SIMON
New York   London   Toronto   Sydney   New Delhi

LITTLE SIMON
An imprint of Simon & Schuster Children's Publishing Division
First Little Simon paperback edition July 2015
1230 Avenue of the Americas, New York, New York 10020
Copyright © 2015 by Simon & Schuster, Inc.
Also available in a Little Simon hardcover edition.
All rights reserved, including the right of reproduction in whole or in part in any form. LITTLE SIMON is a registered trademark of Simon & Schuster, Inc., and associated colophon is a trademark of Simon & Schuster, Inc. For information about special discounts for bulk purchases, please contact Simon & Schuster Special Sales at 1-866-506-1949 or business@simonandschuster.com.
The Simon & Schuster Speakers Bureau can bring authors to your live event. For more information or to book an event contact the Simon & Schuster Speakers Bureau at 1-866-248-3049 or visit our website at www.simonspeakers.com.
Designed by Nick Sciacca
Manufactured in the United States of America 0615 FFG
1 2 3 4 5 6 7 8 9 10
Library of Congress Cataloging-in-Publication Data
O'Ryan, Ray.
A haunted Halloween / by Ray O'Ryan ; illustrated by Jason Kraft. — First edition.
pages cm. — (Galaxy Zack ; #11)
Summary: Although Halloween is not celebrated on the planet Nebulon, Zack, a boy from Earth, discovers that ghosts may be real. —
ISBN 978-1-4814-3490-4 (pbk : alk. paper) —
ISBN 978-1-4814-3491-1 (hc : alk. paper) —
ISBN 978-1-4814-3492-8 (eBook)
[1. Science fiction. 2. Halloween—Fiction. 3. Ghosts—Fiction. 4. Human-alien encounters—Fiction.]
I. Kraft, Jason, illustrator. II. Title.
PZ7.O7843Hau 2015
[Fic]—dc23
2014026721

CONTENTS

Chapter 1
Ghost Stories

Zack Nelson unrolled his sleeping bag on the floor of his friend Drake's bedroom. Zack was at Drake's house for a sleepover. It was Friday night, and Halloween was just a week away!

Zack felt a bit sad. Halloween had been one of his favorite holidays on

Earth. But Zack and his family now lived on the planet Nebulon. On Nebulon, no one had even heard of Halloween!

"So you dress up in costumes?" asked Drake.

Zack had just finished telling Drake all about Halloween.

"Yup," said Zack.

"And you go from house to house, and people give you *free* candy?" Drake asked in disbelief.

"That's right," replied Zack. "And we tell ghost stories too."

"Ghost? What is a ghost?" asked Drake. "I have never heard of it."

"How about I tell you a ghost story?" Zack suggested. "I think that's the best way to explain what they are."

"Sure, I love stories," said Drake.

Drake curled up in his blanket. Zack turned down the light and pulled his sleeping bag over his head. He switched on a small astro-light and placed it under his chin. The glowing metal stick sent a weird shadow across his face.

Zack began his story.

"A family moved into an old house deep in the woods. On their first night in the house, they sat around their table for dinner. Wind whipped through the trees outside. The branches tapped against the windows. An owl hooted in the distance."

Drake pulled his blanket around himself a bit tighter.

Zack continued, "'Can you please pass the salt?' the youngest daughter asked her father. But before her dad could move, the saltshaker rose into the air. It drifted across the table and landed right in front of the little girl."

Drake's eyes opened wide.

Zack saw that his scary story was working. He went on.

"Suddenly an old framed picture flew off the wall. It shot through the air and crashed to the floor!

"'Ghosts!' shouted the little girl.

"And that's when they saw it: A glowing figure appeared above the table, floating in midair. The family could see right through it. Then it vanished in an instant!"

Drake's expression changed from fear to something else.

Zack noticed and stopped his story. "Are you getting too scared, Drake?" he asked. "You don't have to worry. Ghosts aren't real. They're only in stories."

"Oh, I am not scared," Drake said, "just confused. Now that I know what a ghost is. I am sure that they *are* real. In fact, one of them is a good friend of mine!"

Chapter 2
Creep Show

"Very funny, Drake," said Zack. He switched off his astro-light and slipped it into his backpack.

"But I am not kidding, Zack," said Drake. "Ghosts are real, and one is my friend. His name is Hector, and he can do everything you described: float off the ground, disappear, and—"

"Come on, Drake," Zack interrupted.
"Does your friend also happen to be
imaginary?"

Before Drake could respond, Zack
let out a huge yawn. "I think all this
ghost talk has made me sleepy," said
Zack. He nestled into his sleeping bag
and closed his eyes. "Night, Drake!"

The next morning, Zack had breakfast at Drake's house, then headed home.

"Welcome home, Master Just Zack," said Ira, the Nelson's Indoor Robotic Assistant. "How was your sleepover with Master Drake?"

"We had fun," said Zack.

Zack's twin sisters, Cathy and
Charlotte, were sitting at the kitchen
table. They were munching breakfast
and slurping boingoberry smoothies.

"Did you tell Drake . . ."

". . . any scary ghost stories . . ."

". . . from Earth?" the girls asked.

"I tried," said Zack. "But right in the
middle, Drake told me that he believes

in ghosts! Can you believe that? Ghosts aren't real!"

"Shhh. Don't say ghosts . . . ," said Cathy.

". . . aren't real! It's like you're asking them . . . ," Charlotte exclaimed.

". . . to haunt you!" Cathy warned.

Zack laughed. "Now that's the silliest thing I've ever heard!"

Their dad, Otto Nelson, walked into the kitchen.

"What's the silliest thing you ever heard?" he asked. Then he spotted the girls' drinks. "Ohhh, those look good," he said before Zack could answer.

"Ira, I'd like a boingoberry smoothie too, please," said Dad.

"Certainly, Mr. Nelson," said Ira.

A few seconds later, a small panel in the kitchen wall slid open. Out came a bubbling purple drink.

As Dad sipped on his drink, Zack told him about the sleepover.

"Well, you know, Zack, some people believe in ghosts," said Dad. "And

that's okay. Just like it's okay that you
don't. Speaking of ghosts, I've got a
special creepy old vivi-vid picked out
to watch after dinner tonight. I know
you kids miss celebrating Halloween.
I thought this would be fun!"

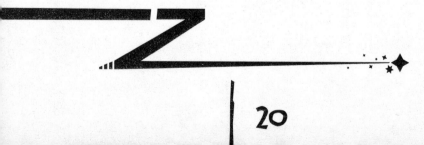

After they ate dinner that evening, the Nelsons settled down in front of their sonic cell monitor. On the living room table sat a big plate of brick bark, a chocolate and plexu-nut snack that Zack had discovered on the planet Plexus.

"This is not going to be too scary for the kids, is it, Otto?" asked Shelly, their mom.

"Nah," said Dad. "I watched this one when *I* was a kid."

The vivi-vid began. A creepy old castle appeared on the sonic cell. Rain poured down. Lightning flashed.

Now THIS feels like Halloween, thought Zack.

Chapter 3
Game Time!

The next afternoon, Zack sat in his room playing Asteroid Blast on his hyperphone.

"Master Just Zack, Master Drake is here," Ira announced.

"Thanks, Ira," said Zack. He saved the game and raced downstairs.

"Hey, Drake. What's zooming?" asked Zack.

"I ran into Seth earlier, and he told me that they have a ton of grape new games at the Starcade," said Drake. "Do you want to go?"

"Yippee wah-wah, you bet I do!" cried Zack. "Starcade games beat handheld hyperphone games any day!"

Zack ran to the kitchen and told his mom where

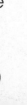

he was headed. Then the boys jumped
on their bikes and rode the few blocks
to the Starcade.

They stepped inside. It felt like they had walked into space. The walls and floor were black. Tiny points of light flickered on the ceiling like stars in the night sky. A glowing green arrow flashed on the floor.

"This way to the . . . STAAAAAR-CAAAAADE!" boomed a loud voice.

Zack and Drake both grinned. Then they followed the blinking arrow.

The two friends stepped into a huge room filled with people playing arcade games. Lights flashed. Bells rang. Buzzers buzzed.

Some voices cheered.
Others moaned. Zack felt as if
he could almost reach out
and touch the excitement.
Soon, Seth joined them.
"Hi, Zack," he said. "Do
you want to play this
grape new game? It is called
Zoom-ber! You get to race
flying cars!"

"Sure!" cried
Zack.

"I have played
it already," said Drake.
"You play with Seth.

I will meet up with you later."

As Drake disappeared around the corner, Zack and Seth slipped into a booth. They took seats behind a large screen. Seth gripped the controls with both hands.

"You steer with the wheel," Seth explained. "The right foot pedal makes you go faster. The left foot pedal slows you down. Ready?"

Zack nodded.

The screen blazed to life. Zack saw two flying cars on the screen in front of him. Zack controlled the yellow car. Seth controlled the red.

"GO!" Seth shouted.

Chapter 4
Bad Luck?

They zoomed along above a gleaming alien city. Zack stepped harder on the go pedal. His car sped in front of Seth's.

The two cars approached a sharp right turn. Zack tried to twist his control to the right. But the wheel suddenly

jerked out of his hand, and his car swung to the left. Seth took the turn smoothly and grabbed the lead.

"What's wrong with this thing?" shouted Zack.

"Nothing, except that you are going to lose!" Seth shot back.

Zack readjusted his course. A few seconds later, his car was right behind Seth's.

"Time to take the lead!" Zack said.

He pressed down hard on the go pedal. His car slowed down.

Did I step on the wrong pedal? Zack wondered. He looked down at his feet.

He was stepping on the right one . . .
but the brake was pushed down too! *It
must have gotten stuck!*

Zack had fallen too far behind to
catch up. Seth's car flew across the
finish line. The Nebulite won the race.

"Told you I would beat you!" Seth said.

"No fair!" Zack cried. "My car was broken!"

"Yeah, sure it was," said Seth. "You are just making excuses. Do not be a sore loser."

Seth headed off to play something else.

Zack looked around but could not find Drake anywhere. He decided to try another game.

Zack was excited to find an arcade-size version of his favorite hyperphone game, Asteroid Blast. He slipped into the game booth. The inside looked like a spaceship. Zack sat down. Screens lit up. Stars flickered all around him.

He gripped the control knob and steered his ship through space.

This is way more grape than the tiny hyperphone version. I really feel like I'm flying!

Suddenly a huge asteroid was right in front of Zack's ship. He aimed the control knob. *Gotcha!* he thought. But as Zack pushed the purple trigger button, the control knob twitched to the right.

POW! POW!

Bright red energy beams shot from the ship. But the blasts flew right past the asteroid. And now the huge chunk of space rock was headed straight for Zack's ship.

He pulled hard on the control knob. His ship turned out of the way at the last second.

Before Zack could catch his breath, another asteroid appeared. Zack tried to aim his laser, but the stick wouldn't budge. He pushed the control knob hard to the right, hoping to dodge the

asteroid. But he felt the control knob suddenly pull back to the left! It was like someone else was working the control!

Why is this happening? Zack wondered. Then the asteroid slammed into his ship.

BWEE! BWEE! BWEE! Game over!
Game over!

Zack climbed out of the booth. He
was frustrated and confused.

That's when Drake showed up.

"Hey, Zack. Ready to go home?" he
asked.

"Yeah," said Zack. "I'm tired of losing. "None of the games I played worked right."

"Hmm," said Drake. "They all worked for me. Maybe the games you tried are haunted! Maybe it was a ghost that was making you lose!" He chuckled.

"Very funny, Drake," replied Zack. "Come on. Let's go."

Chapter 5
Haunted Hallways

That night, Zack replayed the games from the Starcade in his mind over and over. He knew he had made all the right moves. The games were just all broken. What other reason could there be? Ghosts? But he knew that was impossible.

The next day at school, Zack hurried to his locker. The sonic bell chimed in the hallway. Zack was running late for class.

He threw open his locker and grabbed his edu-screen. He was about to reach back in to get his gym uniform when his locker suddenly slammed shut.

Zack had to jump out of the way to avoid getting hit by the locker door.

"Very funny," said Zack. He looked around, expecting to see whoever had slammed the door standing there laughing.

But as Zack glanced down the hall, he realized that no one was near. He opened the door again, snatched the rest of his stuff, and raced off to class.

In gym that day, the students played a game of pulse-ball. Three players from each team tried to control a glowing metal ball. Then they tried to shoot the ball through a moving, flashing hoop that floated in the air.

"Over here!" Seth shouted, waving his hands.

Zack threw the ball to Seth. Seth jumped

into the air and tossed the ball toward the hoop a few feet away. The ball glided smoothly through the hoop.

"All right! One for us!" cried Seth.

Zack gave Seth a high five, a favorite Earth move of Zack's that he had taught his Nebulite friends.

Seth had the glowing ball to start the next play. Zack ran right under the floating hoop.

"Over here!" Zack shouted.

Seth threw the ball right at Zack.

It sped toward him in a straight line.

This is going to be the easiest pulse-bucket of my life! Zack thought.

But just before it reached him, the ball turned sharply to the right. It flew out of bounds.

"What happened?" asked Zack. "It looked like someone knocked the ball away from me. But there was no one there!"

"Duh, you missed the ball, Zack," grumbled Seth. "That is what happened. And it was a good pass too."

Zack shook his head. He just couldn't figure out what was going on.

Later at lunch Zack sat with Drake.

"How is your day going?" asked Drake.

Should I tell him about the locker door and the pulse-ball? Zack thought. *Nah, he'd just say that those things prove he's right about ghosts being real.*

"Pretty good," Zack replied. "How about you?"

"Grape enough," said Drake.

Zack quietly ate the rest of his lunch, lost in thought.

When the school day ended, Zack headed back to his locker. He opened the door, then quickly closed it. He had hoped to catch whoever had slammed it shut earlier—just in case they were back.

No one was there.

Zack slipped his edu-screen and a couple of books into his locker. He was about to close it when his hyperphone

floated from his backpack. Zack watched wide-eyed as the small device drifted through the air down the hall.

Zack ran and snatched the hyperphone out of the air. He slipped it into the side pocket of his backpack. Again,

it drifted out and hung in the air in front of him.

Zack grabbed the phone again and then went back to close his locker.

Maybe Drake is right, he thought. *Maybe ghosts are real!*

Chapter 6
Bert to the Rescue

That night, Zack was unusually quiet.

"How was school today, honey?" asked his mom.

Zack shrugged. "Okay," he said. He wasn't ready to tell his family about the weird stuff that had been happening to him. And he certainly wasn't ready to tell anybody that he was starting to believe that ghosts might be real.

After dinner, Zack tried to play another game of Asteroid Blast on his hyperphone. But he had trouble concentrating. His spaceship was soon destroyed in a collision with a giant asteroid.

"I have to talk to somebody about this," Zack said aloud. "I can't talk to Drake. I don't want to tell my family. But . . . wait a minute. Bert! I can talk to Bert about anything."

Bert was Zack's best friend on Earth.

Zack punched Bert's galactic code into his hyperphone. Then a few seconds later a face appeared on the screen—a blue face with pointed ears. It was the face of a Nebulite.

"Oh, sorry, I must have entered the wrong galactic code, I was—"

"No, Zack. It's me!" said the blue person on the screen. "It's Bert! I decided to dress up as a Nebulite for Halloween! I was just trying out my costume."

The two friends laughed. Zack had known that just talking with Bert would make him feel better.

"Well, you sure fooled me!" he said. "That's a great costume! Did you know that they don't celebrate Halloween on Nebulon? I've been telling Drake all about it."

"Wow!" said Bert. "I'll miss you this Halloween. When we went trick-or-treating together, it was always fun. Even if we had to take my little sisters along. This year Roberta and Darlene are dressing up as ghosts. It's pretty great."

"Ghosts!" exclaimed Zack. "That's why I called you in the first place! This is going to sound really strange, but I think I'm being haunted!"

Zack filled Bert in on all the weird stuff that had been going on.

"But why would ghosts haunt you, Zack?" Bert asked.

"I have no idea," said Zack. "Unless it's because they got mad when I told Drake that I don't believe in them."

"Maybe. I wonder what the best way to get rid of them is," Bert thought aloud.

That's when Zack remembered the
scary vivi-vid he'd watched with his
family.

"Maybe the ghost has to tell me some-thing," said Zack. "In a vivi-vid I just saw, a ghost wanted some bad guys to leave the house he loved. After they left, the ghost stopped haunting the place."

"Makes sense to me," said Bert.

"Thanks, Bert!" said Zack. "I think we've figured it out: The best way to get rid of a ghost is to give it what it wants. Now all I have to do is figure out what that is!"

Chapter 7
Drake's Answer

The next day at school, Zack was distracted. He kept trying to figure out what the ghost wanted from him. He came up with nothing.

"Zack?" asked a voice that sounded very far away.

Oh no! Zack thought. *Could the*

ghost be calling my name?

"Zack?" the voice said again.

Zack quickly realized that the voice belonged to his teacher, Ms. Rudolph. She was trying to ask him a question.

"Yes, Ms. Rudolph?" Zack said, embarrassed that he hadn't been paying attention.

"Can you please tell the class which of Nebulon's three moons was explored first?" Ms. Rudolph asked.

"Tratell," replied Zack.

"Correct," Ms. Rudolph said, "and I'd like it if you would pay more attention in class."

"Yes, Ms. Rudolph," said Zack. His face was bright red.

After school, Zack hopped on his bike and headed for home. He was glad he had decided to ride to school that day. It gave him time to think. As he pedaled, he thought about what he'd be doing if he were celebrating Halloween back on Earth.

I'd be dressing up in a cool costume. I'd go trick-or-treating with Bert and get tons of candy. And the only ghosts I'd have to worry about would be Bert's sisters in their costumes!

Zack stopped his bike.

That does it! he thought. *I have to talk to Drake about this ghost stuff. I can't think of anything else, and it's starting to mess me up at school!*

He quickly turned around and headed for Drake's. A short time later, he hopped off his bike and stepped up to Drake's front door.

"Good afternoon, Master Zack," said the Ira at Drake's house. "I'll let Master Drake know you're here."

"Thanks, Ira," said Zack.

A few seconds later, Drake opened the front door.

"Hi, Zack," he said. "I did not expect you."

"I know," said Zack. "Listen, I'm
sorry I said that ghosts aren't real.
I didn't mean to make fun of you for
believing in them. In fact, now I think
you are right. Not only do I believe in
ghosts, but I think I'm actually being
haunted by one."

"Really?" said Drake. "Tell me what happened."

Drake stepped outside. The two friends sat down on a force-bench on Drake's porch. The glowing blue bench was created by an energy field. When Zack sat on the bench, he felt as if he were floating on a cloud.

"First, I lost every game I played at the Starcade," Zack explained, "but not because I wasn't playing well. The ghost stepped on the wrong pedal in Zoom-ber! Then the ghost messed up my aim in Asteroid Blast."

Drake just nodded and listened.

"Then, at school, my locker door slammed shut by itself. When I was playing pulse-ball,

80

the ghost knocked away a perfect pass from Seth. And my hyperphone floated out of my backpack."

"Hmm...," Drake said.

"So here's what I think: The ghost wants something from me. If I can just figure out what it wants and make it happy, then it will leave me alone."

Drake smiled and laughed softly.

"You are right, Zack," he said. "The *ghost* does want something from you. And I know exactly what it is."

Chapter 8
A Ghostly Explanation

Zack was stunned.

"How on Nebulon do you know what the ghost wants?" Zack asked. "And what *does* it want? Halloween candy? My hyperphone? To win a few games?"

"No, Zack," said Drake. "I think the ghost just wants you to believe him when he tells you something."

Zack shook his head. "What do you mean?" he asked.

Drake reached into his back pocket. He pulled out what looked like a small black stick.

"Zack, *I* am the one that has been haunting you!" said Drake.

Drake pressed a button on the black stick. He pointed it at a large rock. When Drake moved the stick up, the rock rose into the air. When he moved the stick to the right, the rock moved to the right.

"This is an auto-matter mover," Drake explained. "If I push this button and aim it at something, I can move any object."

"That's why I couldn't win at the Starcade!" said Zack.

"Yes," said Drake. "I was hiding at the Starcade and at school. I used the auto-matter mover to move the game controls. I also made the locker slam and the ball move and your hyper-phone float too."

"That is amazing!" said Zack.

"I hope you are not mad at me for fooling you like that, Zack," said Drake. "I was upset that you did not believe me when I said that ghosts are real."

"I'm not mad," said Zack. "I just can't believe that you were able to fool me like that!"

Drake smiled and turned off his auto-matter mover.

"So, wait a minute," Zack said suddenly. "You were pretending to be the ghost. And you were using that device to trick me. That means ghosts *aren't* real, and I was right all along!"

"Well, no, not exactly," said Drake. "When you described ghosts to me the other night, I told you

that I knew someone who could do all those things, remember?"

"Yeah, I guess I remember," said Zack. "But—"

"Well, I am trying to get my parents to take us to visit this 'ghost' next Saturday," said Drake. "He is actually my friend Hector who lives on the planet Spektor."

"Oh, so he's an alien—an alien who *looks* like a ghost! Why didn't you say so? And Saturday is Halloween," said Zack. "It's perfect! I'll check with my parents to see if I can go."

Chapter 9
Permission Granted!

As soon as Zack got home, he asked his parents if he could go to Spektor with Drake.

"Are Drake's parents going?" asked Mom.

"Yup," replied Zack. "In fact, Drake's parents and Hector's parents are old

friends. They're looking forward to the visit as much as we are."

"I've never been to Spektor," said Dad, pulling out a galactic map. "But I hear it's a strange-looking planet. Could be perfect for Halloween."

"Okay," said Mom. "But I'd still like you to have your hyperphone on the whole time, okay?"

"Sure! Thanks, Mom!"

Zack had to tell Bert. He hurried to his room and punched Bert's galactic code into his hyperphone. This time,

Bert's familiar face appeared on Zack's screen. "More ghosts?" asked Bert, smiling. "Nah," said Zack. "I know they're not real."

"Then who messed up your Starcade games and the pulse-ball pass?" Bert asked.

"It was Drake!" Zack explained. "He was using an auto-matter mover. He was just upset that I didn't believe him when he said he knew a ghost. Turns out that what he thought was a ghost is really his friend Hector, an alien from the planet Spektor."

"So, Hector looks like a ghost?" asked Bert.

"Exactly!" said Zack. "And, best of all, Drake and I are going to visit Hector on Halloween!"

"Be sure to z-mail me vids of you guys with Hector!" said Bert.

"And you have to send me vids of
you trick-or-treating as a Nebulite!"
Zack said.

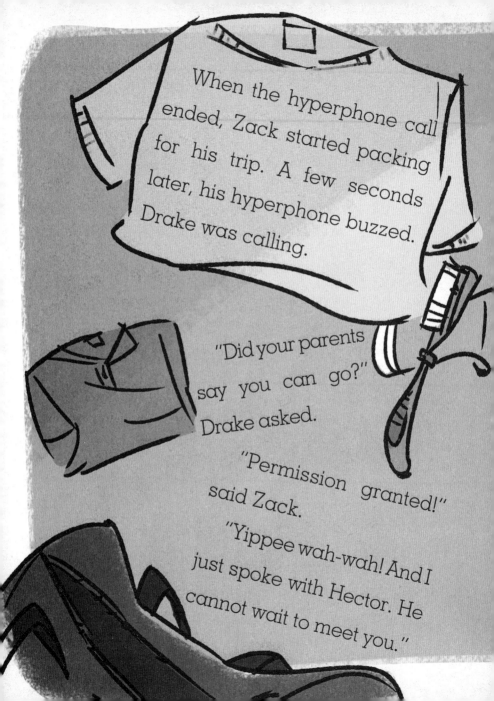

When the hyperphone call ended, Zack started packing for his trip. A few seconds later, his hyperphone buzzed. Drake was calling.

"Did your parents say you can go?" Drake asked.

"Permission granted!" said Zack.

"Yippee wah-wah! And I just spoke with Hector. He cannot wait to meet you."

Chapter 10

Hector, from Spektor

Halloween finally arrived. Zack, Drake, and Drake's parents boarded the shuttle from Nebulon to Spektor.

"I cannot wait for you to meet Hector and see his planet," said Drake.

"Me too!" said Zack.

"You know, I used to work with

Hector's mom, Zack," said Mrs. Taylor, Drake's mother. "I cannot tell you how many times she scared me when she popped out of nowhere."

"They can really do that?" asked Zack in awe.

After a short trip, the shuttle dropped out of ultra-speed. Zack looked out the window and saw a planet below. Gray clouds swirled above the planet's surface.

"Looks kinda gloomy," said Zack.

"Perfect for Halloween, right?" said Drake.

The shuttle landed at the spaceport. Zack and Drake walked into the terminal. Zack's eyes opened wide at what he saw.

The people on Spektor really did look like ghosts! They shimmered with a light-blue glow. They floated just above the ground as they moved around the terminal. And Zack could see right through them!

"There are Hector and his parents!" shouted Drake.

Zack, Drake, and Mr. and Mrs. Taylor walked over to three glowing figures.

"How lovely to see you again, Adora!" said Hector's mother. She hugged Drake's mom. Zack could see Mrs. Taylor's body right through her transparent arms.

"Well, you must be Drake's new friend Zack," said the glowing figure floating next to Hector's mom. "I'm Ramek, Hector's dad."

"Nice to meet you, sir," said Zack. He glanced down and tried to spot Ramek's feet. He had none. He hovered above the ground.

"And this," Drake said, pointing toward the smallest of the three glowing figures, "is my friend. The one and ghostly, Hector!"

Zack lifted his hand in front of his face and started to move it in a small circle. This was the way Nebulites said hello. But when Zack looked over, Hector was gone. He had simply vanished into thin air.

Suddenly, Zack felt someone tap him on the back. He jumped in surprise, then turned around. There was no one standing behind him.

Zack turned back around. There was
Hector, standing next to his parents.

"Boo!" shouted Hector.

"Now, Hector, you know it's impolite
to tease people," said Hector's mom.

"How did you do that?" Zack asked.
Thanks to Mrs. Taylor's warning, he

wasn't scared. Though he was impressed.

"You mean this?" asked Hector.

Hector disappeared right in front of Zack's eyes. Once again, Zack felt a tap on his back. He turned around and saw nothing. Then Hector slowly appeared.

"Hector!" scolded his father. "What did your mother just say?"

"Sorry. Drake told me about Halloween ghosts, so I watched some old scary movies from Earth," Hector explained. "I think I'd make a great ghost!"

Zack laughed, and Hector's dad rolled his glowing green eyes. "Now who wants a tour of Spektor?" he asked.

"Me!" said Zack.

The whole group set out for a tour of Spektor. As they walked from the spaceport, Zack saw that the entire planet looked gray. Fog swirled through the air. Everywhere Zack looked, shimmering figures floated along the sidewalks.

"I couldn't think of a better place to spend Halloween," Zack said, smiling.

Drake smiled too.

"And I'm sorry again that I didn't believe you, Drake," Zack said.

"Do not worry," said Drake. "It is time to have the best Halloween ever!"

GALAXY ZACK

ADVENTURE!

HERE'S A SNEAK PEEK!

It was family game night at the Nelson house. Zack and Drake were one team. Charlotte and Cathy were another. And their parents were the third team.

Zack pinned his arms at his sides. He began to jump up and down.

"Jump!" guessed Drake.

An excerpt from *Operation Twin Trouble!*

Zack shook his head.

"Bounce!" Drake shouted.

Zack stopped jumping and cupped his hand behind his ear.

"Sounds like bounce?"

Next, Zack held his hands together over his head.

"Circle?" guessed Drake. "Zero? . . . The letter O?"

Zack touched his nose, the sign that Drake was correct.

"Bounce-O-what?"

Zack pretended he had a shovel in his hands and was digging in the ground. Then he pretended to throw something into the imaginary hole.

"Bury!" shouted Drake.

Again, Zack touched his nose.

"Bounce-O-Bury," Drake said. He thought for moment. "Boingoberry!"

"That's it!" yelled Zack. He gave Drake a high five.

Boingoberries grew all over Venus. They were used to make Zack's favorite shake and syrup.

Drake looked at the timer hologram. "One minute and thirty seconds," he announced. "Pretty good."

"Okay, girls. Your turn," Zack said.

The girls stood up. They both had

flaming red hair. Charlotte kept hers in a ponytail. She also wore a scarf around her neck. Cathy wore her hair in two braided pigtails. This was the only way most people could tell them apart.

"Ready, set, go!" Zack shouted.

Charlotte stuck her left hand out. She then pretended to strum a guitar with her right hand.

"TBD!" Cathy shouted.

"That's it!" Charlotte said. She glanced up at the timer. "Five seconds! A new record!"

Zack jumped up. "TBD? That's not even a word!"

"Shows what you know. TBD is . . ."

". . . our favorite band. It stands for . . ."

". . . Twin Boys Dancing!"

"I have heard of TBD," said Drake. "In fact, I read that they are playing a concert on their home planet, Mirer.

The girls ran over to their parents.

"Can we . . ."

". . . go . . ."

". . . please?"

"Well," said Mrs. Nelson, "I guess that would be okay."

"Yay!" the girls screeched.

Mr. Nelson scratched his head. "But what about our turn?"

An excerpt from *Operation Twin Trouble!*